A Boy and a Boa

A
Boy and a Boa

by ABBY ISRAEL

pictures by Kevin Brooks

The Dial Press   New York

Published by The Dial Press
1 Dag Hammarskjold Plaza
New York, New York 10017

Based on *A Boy and a Boa* produced by
Lora Hays and Renata Stoia for Boa Films.
Executive Producer, New York State Education
Department. Segments from the Vegetable Soup
series. Copyright 1975 by the New York State
Education Department. All rights reserved.

Library of Congress Cataloging in Publication Data

Israel, Abigail P / A boy and a boa.

Summary/When Marvin's pet boa constrictor gets loose
in the library, Marvin and his friends begin a frantic pursuit.
[1. Boa constrictor–Fiction. 2. Snakes as pets–Fiction.
3. Libraries–Fiction] I. Brooks, Kevin. II. Title.
PZ7.I84Bo   [Fic]   80-25812
ISBN 0-8037-0708-8
ISBN 0-8037-0716-9 (lib. bdg.)

For Elie

CHAPTER

1

"Martin, you get that thing out of here right away!"

Martin's mother upset the basket of vegetables on the table and retreated to the far end of the kitchen. It was a large kitchen, longer than it was wide. A row of gleaming copper-bottomed pots and pans hung from the far wall. There were blue-and-white tiles on the floor, and blue-and-white checkered curtains at the big window above the sink. In the middle of the room a square table was strewn with carrots and onions and green peppers and tomatoes and big white mushrooms waiting to be chopped.

[7]

Martin gently lowered the aquarium onto the table, next to the carrots, and looked up. He knew perfectly well why his mother was so upset—after all, he didn't exactly have fish in that aquarium. But on the other hand, he found all the fuss pretty ridiculous.

"Now, Mom, it's all right," he said soothingly. "There's nothing to worry about. You'll love him. I know you will!"

"Love that *thing*? I'll *never* love that thing!"

"Of course you will, Mom. Lots of people do. He's not a brontosaurus, you know. I'm not asking you to love a brontosaurus!"

"A brontosaurus would be easier, Martin," his mother protested. "At least they stay outside, and you don't have any trouble finding them when you want them. And anyway, they're extinct!"

Martin stared at the plants that sat on the windowsill. There were pots of herbs and cacti and radish plants and sprouts and little flowering tubs whose names he could never remember. His mother was a terrific gardener.

"Brontosauruses aren't pets, Mom," he said finally. *"Pets!"*

"That's what I've been trying to tell you," said Martin. "This is Nigel. He's my new pet."

[8]

Martin's mother backed up against the refrigerator. She was a tall woman with a fabulous Afro, a wide smile, and a dimple in each cheek. She worked in a real estate office downtown and had a reputation for never letting anything ruffle her feathers. But right now nothing was going to get her out of the safety zone.

"You mean you brought it from school and you're going to take care of it over spring vacation?" she asked hopefully. "Well, perhaps we can manage that if you—"

"Mom," Martin interrupted. "Nigel's not an 'it.' He's a he. And he's not from school. Nigel's mine," he went on cautiously. "I bought him with my own money, the money I saved from baby-sitting. Dad came with me to the pet store. He even helped me pick him out."

Martin was ten years old and tall for his age. He had a broad smile like his mother's, although right now he was frowning. The situation did not look promising. He unzipped his baseball jacket, stuck his hands in the pockets of his jeans, and stared at his sneakers.

"Oh, Tom, how could you!" Martin's mother exclaimed. "I mean, why did you let him? I mean, we can't have a . . . a *snake* in the house!"

"Of course we can, Gloria," Martin's father said, smiling. He hadn't said a word since they'd brought Nigel inside, but now he felt Martin could use a little help. "There's absolutely nothing to worry about—"

"How do you know?" Martin's mother interrupted. "You don't know what goes on in the head of a creature like that."

Nigel had woken up and was looking out at his new surroundings. The inspection made Martin's mother even more nervous.

"No, I don't have the foggiest idea what goes on in Nigel's head, dear," Martin's father said, laughing. "But with all this commotion, I'd imagine he's wondering what sort of zoo he's in now!"

Nigel turned his head and stared at Martin's father.

"You see!" Martin's mother exclaimed, folding her arms emphatically across her chest. "He heard you. He's probably plotting something already!"

"Mom," said Martin, trying to be patient. "Snakes don't hear well at all. In fact, they're probably deaf. What turns them on is vibrations. And it seems to me the vibrations in this kitchen—"

"Really, Gloria," Martin's father hastened to intervene, putting his doctor's bag on the chair. "I've studied the whole question, and I promise you there's nothing difficult about having a pet snake. They're clean, they're quiet, they're beautiful, they're—"

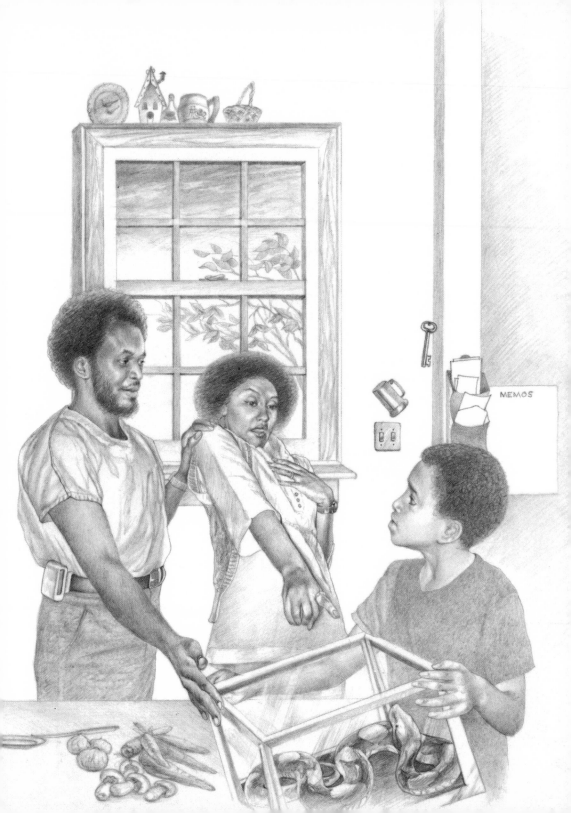

"*Beautiful!*" Martin's mother echoed, raising her arms to the ceiling. "Do you really think *that's* beautiful?"

Martin had taken the top off Nigel's aquarium and was lifting him out, very carefully. Martin's mother shrank back against the refrigerator again.

"Look at the colors, Mom. He's just finished shedding. That's when his colors are the brightest."

The boa seemed to be examining the scene. Martin's father gingerly gave him a little pat.

"You'll see," he said slowly. "Nigel will be part of the family in no time."

"That's what I'm afraid of," Martin's mother sighed, shaking her head. "I admit he's rather handsome—in his own way, that is. But I don't see why *we* have to be the only people on the block with a snake in the family."

"Nigel's not just a snake, Mom," Martin objected, as Nigel slowly wrapped himself around his arm. "He's the King of Snakes! He's a boa constrictor!"

Martin and his father smiled at each other. Nigel settled himself comfortably into position and went back to sleep. Martin's mother edged forward.

"But where did you learn about boa constrictors?" she asked. "I mean, who taught you all that?"

"Scot did," Martin answered with a big smile. "You

know—the guy who's curator at the Children's Zoo. I see him almost every time I go. He's really terrific with animals, and I guess he just took a liking to me. Anyway, it's a little bit your fault. I asked Scot a lot of questions about boas because it looked like a snake might just be the one animal you and Dad would let me have."

"A boa constrictor the one animal we'd let you have?" Martin's mother repeated, opening her eyes wide. "Where did you ever get *that* idea?"

"Because the great thing about boas," Martin replied, "is you don't have to walk them, you don't have to buy kitty litter, they don't wake the neighbors up in the middle of the night, they don't turn over trash cans or dig up people's lawns, and they only eat about once a month. Except that Nigel won't eat spotted mice. He's very fussy."

"Mice?" Martin's mother cried, backing up to the refrigerator again.

"Martin," his father said gently. "Why don't you take Nigel up to your room while I talk to your mother? Just make sure he stays in the aquarium. Things are complicated enough as they are."

"Okay, Dad," Martin said, lowering Nigel into his glass house. There was a faint smile on his lips as he

[13]

pictured the scene between his parents. "Just don't worry, Mom. You'll get used to Nigel a lot faster than you'd get used to a brontosaurus!"

"I'll *never* get used to that thing!" Martin's mother exclaimed, finally letting go of the refrigerator when she saw that Nigel was on his way out of the room. "It's so big and so silent and so . . . well so . . . *different*."

"Oh, Mom," Martin sighed, pausing at the doorway. "You're so prejudiced. You don't even *know* him yet!"

CHAPTER

2

The next morning, after breakfast, Martin was on his way upstairs to check on Nigel when he happened to glance through the living room window. About half a dozen of his friends were coming up the front walk. They looked alarmingly like a delegation, and Martin thought he'd better go out and deal with the situation head-on. His mother was always telling him how fast news travels around a block. He was sure he knew what they'd come for.

"Hi, gang!" he said casually from the top step. "What's up?"

The gang looked up at him, suddenly unsure of themselves. There were eight of them, not counting Martin, and they'd all been best friends since the first grade. They all lived on Martin's street, and went to Charlton Elementary School just four blocks away. All except for little Peter. He was only five, and still in kindergarten.

Eli, Martin's best friend, stepped forward. He was tall, and had curly red hair and the biggest feet in the gang. His ever-present Yankee cap perched precariously over one ear. Martin thought he looked a little embarrassed.

"Martin," Eli began, clearing his throat. "We think you should know . . . I mean, well, my dad doesn't like the idea of a poisonous snake on the block, you know!"

Martin sighed. It was hard enough coping with his mother, but now he had to deal with everyone else's parents as well.

"Don't be stupid, Eli—"

But Martin never got to explain that boa constrictors weren't poisonous, because everyone started shouting at the same time.

"Yeah!" Bob yelled, swinging the stetson hat his mother had brought back for him from her trip to Texas. "My mom says it'll give the block a bad reputation if the news gets out!"

"My grandmother heard this story about a snake that got loose in some guy's bathroom . . ." Dorothy began, pushing up her glasses. They always slipped down her nose when she got excited.

"Why don'tcha get a dog like a normal person!" Eileen called, jumping up and down, her long blond ponytail spraying out behind her like a waterfall.

"My brother says you'll get squeezed to death!" Peter chimed in, trying to free the plastic sword that had gotten caught in his belt.

"It's dis-*gust*-ing, Martin!" Laura and Lucy chorused. They lived right across the street from Martin, and no one could tell them apart. Their mother made them wear different-colored T-shirts, but the girls always switched them back and forth until nobody knew who was who. Right now they were both wearing yellow corduroy overalls. Lucy had a blue T-shirt and Laura a green one, although that was not the way they'd started out.

Martin just stared at them all. He was astonished. Finally he shrugged his shoulders and let out a piercing whistle through his front teeth. Everyone fell silent.

"Look, you don't even know what you're talking about! Why don't you come up to my room and see him? If he's not sleeping, I'll even let you hold him. You can go first, Peter. And then anyone else who wants to can have a turn, okay?"

"Ooooooooh," squealed Laura and Lucy, clasping hands. "He'll be all slimy!"

"Nigel's a lot of things," Martin said crossly, "but slimy he's not. Come on!"

After a little hesitation his friends followed Martin inside and up the stairs. Nigel was wide awake and exploring his aquarium. Everyone crowded around.

"Why's he keep flicking his tongue like that?" Bob asked warily. Bob not only had the loudest voice, he was the oldest and always asked questions first. "He looks scary."

"He looks like he thinks he's Dracula," Lucy said, nervously clutching one of her long black pigtails.

"That's the way snakes get their sense of direction," Martin said. "It doesn't mean he wants to bite you."

"I don't really *have* to hold him, you know," little Peter said, edging away from the front lines and chewing on his plastic sword. "I'm sure it feels good, though. Why don't you do it, Bob? You can have my turn."

"No one *has* to hold him," Martin said. "I mean, Nigel's not a toy. I just thought you'd like to find out for yourselves that he's not a monster from outer space!"

"I'm not afraid," Dorothy said bravely, straightening her shoulders and pushing up her glasses. "He doesn't even look slimy. Maybe I'll try it. Just for a second."

Martin gently lifted Nigel out of the aquarium and handed him to Dorothy. Nigel seemed to like her blue angora sweater, because he curled himself happily around her arm right away.

"Oh!" Dorothy exclaimed. "He's dry!"

"Watch out he doesn't give you the big squeeze, Dorothy!" Eli shouted, dancing around on one foot.

Nigel turned his head and stared at Eli. Eli stared back, then came closer and gave him a cautious pat on the back.

"He feels nice," Dorothy said to Martin. "But is he going to grow a lot?"

"Depends on how much we feed him," Martin answered. "Right now he's about four feet long. When he's all grown up, he'll probably be about six feet."

"That's as tall as my daddy!" Peter shouted.

Everyone laughed and gathered around Dorothy. Now they all wanted to touch Nigel.

"Do you let him sleep with you?" Laura asked.

"Well, that's not—" Martin began.

"Can we give him a bath?"

"He doesn't—"

"How does he get untangled?"

"He just—"

"Can he see in the dark?"

"Not—"

"Well, what *does* he eat?"

The questions came pouring out all at once, and Martin couldn't get in any answers. He was just about to try another of his famous whistles and explain where he planned to get Nigel's mice when his mother called him.

"You're wanted on the phone, Martin!"

Martin hoped it was nobody's father or mother. He wanted to set the record straight with the kids first. Quickly he took Nigel from Dorothy and put him back in the aquarium.

"Okay, everybody," he said. "You can look, but don't touch until I get back. And I think Nigel would appreciate a little peace and quiet."

Martin ran downstairs and picked up the phone. It was Scot from the Children's Zoo. He'd already heard about Nigel from his friend who owned the pet store, and he wanted to ask Martin a favor.

"Listen, Martin," he said. "I've got a real problem here. Our boa, Patty, is about to shed, and you know how their eyes cloud over and they get cranky when that happens. Would it be okay if I borrowed Nigel for the zoo show at the library this afternoon? Everyone will be disappointed if there's no boa constrictor."

"Hey! I've only had him one day and already he's a star!" Martin shouted excitedly. "Sure you can borrow him."

"It's a special show, you know," Scot went on. "I'm bringing in a lot of reptiles from the zoo to show the kids. The library is setting up the big basement room for us. It looks like a lot of people are coming. In fact, if there's a big crowd, maybe you could help me with the show, all right?"

"Sure! Fine! Wow!" Martin said, trying not to sound too excited. He liked Scot a lot and was flattered at the invitation. Scot had told him last summer that he had a real talent for handling animals.

Martin raced back upstairs to tell the gang.

"But, Martin," said Dorothy, ever practical. "What are you going to carry him in? The aquarium's pretty heavy, and when people see what's inside, you can be sure there'll be an awful traffic jam!"

"You can have my rabbit cage," Peter offered eagerly. "I'll just let the rabbits hop around the house till you get back."

"Thanks, Peter," said Martin. "But Nigel could get out of it too easily."

"Yeah," said Eli, taking off his Yankee cap and scratching his head. "He could catch a cold, too."

"How about your father's briefcase?" said Laura.

"Or a suitcase!" said Lucy.

"Maybe a pillowcase?" Bob speculated.

"You could use a shopping bag," said Eileen. "That's how I got my guinea pig to the vet last week."

"Or a school bag," said Laura.

"Or a golf bag!" shouted Peter. "My father has—"

"Please, Peter," Martin interrupted. "Why don't we just leave the parents out of this one? I don't think your father'd like the idea of a snake in his golf clubs."

[23]

"Well, what about a lunch box?" said Lucy.

"Or a hatbox!" Peter tried again. "My sister has—"

"I've got it!" Martin shouted, cutting Peter off before he went through every member of his family. "I'll use my bowling bag! No one pays any attention to bowling bags."

Everyone agreed that this was a pretty good solution, so Martin lifted Nigel out of the aquarium and settled him inside the bowling bag. Nigel curled up immediately and went back to sleep. Martin zipped up the bag, careful to leave a small space so that Nigel would get plenty of air, called good-bye to his mother, and while the gang rushed to their houses to ask if they could go to the zoo show, he began walking to the library.

CHAPTER

3

The local library was six blocks from Martin's house. On his way, he passed a great many neighbors and friends and storekeepers, but no one even looked twice at his bag.

The library was a grand old stone building with a wrought-iron clock tower on the roof, tall columns in front, and a wide set of steps leading up to the door. The railing was polished brass and made a terrific sliding pole.

As Martin started up the steps, a boy came zooming down the railing, hopped off just before the end, and

[25]

crashed headlong into Martin. Martin sat down heavily on the bottom step. The bowling bag flew out of his hand and landed halfway up the steps.

"Whatcha got there?" the slider asked, pointing to the bag.

"Just my bowling bag," Martin answered guardedly, picking himself up. The slider was older than he was, and taller, and looked a lot meaner.

"Just your bowling bag, huh, kid?" shouted a boy in a bright green headband, who'd been waiting with a friend for his turn to slide down the railing. Both boys raced down the steps and grabbed the bag before Martin could get to it.

"Little light for a bowling bag, don'tcha think?" the boy with the headband called. "What you got in it?"

The three boys had formed a wide semicircle around Martin. He looked at them nervously. He could feel the tension in the air as the tallest boy called down:

"I asked you a question, kid! What you got in it?"

"Well . . ." Martin hesitated. "Well . . . actually, it's a snake."

"A *snake*!" all three boys chorused. "A SNAAA-AAAKE!"

"Yes," Martin said. "A snake. Really."

"Well, whaddaya know!" the boy with the headband

[26]

jeered. "Hey, Raoul! The kid says he's got a biiig fat old snake in the little bitty bag! Who d'ya think you're kidding, kid? You got a snake in here just like I got a dinosaur in my pocket!"

"Maybe we should open it up and find out!" Raoul yelled, laughing. "Pass it down here, Saul baby!"

Saul threw the bag to Raoul, who shrieked and tossed it down to the slider. Martin stood by helplessly. Three against one was pretty poor odds. They were charging up and down the steps, running circles around him.

Suddenly he realized that if he could just get into the library, maybe he could get Scot to help him. But when he tried to sneak past them, the slider tripped him and he fell down again. The bowling bag landed in Saul's arms, and Saul disappeared with it into the library.

While Raoul and the slider laughed and cheered, Martin managed to slip into the library. They were so busy talking about him and his imaginary snake they never noticed he'd gone.

Once safely inside, Martin looked around in dismay. It was so quiet he could hear his heart pounding. The only noise came from an old man who'd dozed off over his newspaper and was snoring like Rip Van Winkle. He strained his ears for the sound of running footsteps, but heard nothing. The vaulted ceiling was three stories high and painted with beautiful jungle scenes. Martin wondered if Nigel would like them. Then he looked up at the three levels of library stacks. How would he ever be able to find anything in all those books? And where should he begin?

While Martin was trying to decide on a strategy, Saul had found an empty corner on the third floor and had crawled behind a table to examine his loot. As he un-

zipped the bowling bag, he giggled to himself. That dumb kid, telling me he's got a snake in a bowling bag, he thought.

The zipper stuck partway, so he reached inside—and almost jumped out of his skin.

"Holy Granoly!" Saul couldn't help shouting. He jumped up, dropped the bag, and rushed out of the stacks. When he got to the stairs, he skidded to a stop and peered around. He'd have to sneak out without anyone seeing him or he'd be in big trouble. He crept down the two flights of stairs, then slipped behind the card catalog just as the librarian came up to Martin.

"Are you looking for something special, young man?" she asked, adjusting her spectacles.

"Ah . . . well, no thank you," Martin stammered, looking around wildly. "I mean . . . well, it's just that I lost . . . well, you see . . ."

As Martin tried to figure out how to tell the librarian about Nigel, Saul ducked out the door and took off around the corner. Martin never even saw him go.

"It's all right, young man," said the librarian, patting him on the shoulder. "Just you calm down and tell me all about it. What did you lose?"

"Well, I didn't exactly *lose* it," Martin tried again. "It's just that I had this bowling bag . . ."

"Bowling bag?" the librarian echoed, looking at Martin closely over the top of her glasses.

"Uh . . . yes," said Martin. "Bowling bag."

"Where did you lose it?" the librarian asked, raising her eyebrows.

Martin felt as if he were skating on very thin ice. How could he have gotten himself into such a mess? He wished he'd been braver outside. Of course, he *could* tell her that he hadn't come to the library to bowl but to lend Scot a boa constrictor for the zoo show. On the other hand, he felt it might be easier all around if he just kept his mouth shut and didn't specify what was in the bag. Everybody seemed awfully touchy when it came to snakes.

"I can't remember where I was," he said nervously. "I mean, I was in a lot of different sections. But it's a dark brown bag with a red handle."

"Don't you worry, young man," the librarian said soothingly. "I'm sure we can find it. Why don't you go down to the basement auditorium while we look for it? There's a man from the zoo down there doing a wonderful animal show. He told me they even had a boa constrictor! Can you imagine that? Now go on, and I'll bring you the bag as soon as we have it."

"Thank you," Martin said in a small voice. He wanted

to look for the bag himself, but he thought he'd better go downstairs first and tell Scot about the delay. Maybe he could stretch out the show until they could locate the star.

CHAPTER

4

Martin saw the whole gang as soon as he entered the big basement room. They were sitting together in the outer circle of chairs facing the door. He saw Scot, too. The zoo caretaker was wearing his bright orange-and-white uniform with the initials CCZ (Charlton County Zoo) on the right-hand pocket.

Scot had set up all his animals in their cages on tables in the middle of the room and had arranged the chairs in a double circle around him so that everyone could see easily. The room was full; every seat was taken, and there were a lot of grown-ups and older kids standing behind the second circle of chairs.

"This, my friends, is called an arboreal lizard," Scot was saying, as he walked around the inner circle holding up a scaly creature with strange hard tufts on its back.

The children squealed. One little girl stood up and put her hand out hesitantly. Everyone cheered.

"And this," Scot went on, putting the lizard back into its cage and picking up what looked to Martin like a miniature green dragon, "—this is an iguana. We call her Baby Godzilla, but her tail is actually twice as long as her body. She's very big on strawberries and bananas."

"How about spinach?" shouted little Peter, bobbing up and down excitedly in his seat, holding his plastic sword.

"Loves it!" Scot told him. "And lettuce and watercress, and this morning she even put away some brussels sprouts!"

"Yecchh," Eli groaned.

"Honestly, Eli," said Dorothy, looking at him severely. "When are you going to grow up? This is a serious show!"

Martin stood in the doorway and thought hard. He couldn't bring himself to interrupt the performance.

Luckily, Scot had brought a lot of animals. Perhaps he still had time to find Nigel before the last act.

Suddenly he had a brilliant idea. If he could just signal to the gang and get them out of the room without attracting attention, he could organize a real search party. With all of them combing the stacks, someone was sure to spot Nigel.

"Now this," Scot was saying, "is a Carolina anole. She changes colors when the temperature goes up or down. . . ."

Martin waited for Scot to turn toward the back of the room, then waved his arms and hoped one of the gang would get the message. Finally, Lucy and Laura noticed him on their way up to feed the iguana a radish top. Quietly, they made their way over to him.

"Hey, Martin!" they chorused. "Where's Nigel?"

"Shhhh," Martin hissed, glancing around. "Listen, I've got a big problem and I need your help. Can you get the rest of the kids together without making a big production out of it and meet me upstairs on the . . . uh . . . the third floor?"

"But what—?" Lucy began.

"Not now," Martin whispered. "Please, just do what I said and I'll explain everything later. I'll meet you upstairs in five minutes. Now hurry up!"

Meanwhile, up on the third floor, Nigel was doing some investigating of his own. While Lucy and Laura were gathering the gang together, he poked his head out of Martin's bowling bag. Slowly he slithered out of the bag and into the nearest corner. A nice warm dark corner was just what he needed. In fact, with all the shelves and tables and chairs and books, he had an endless number of corners to choose from!

At the opposite end of the third floor, Martin marshaled his troops.

"Okay, let's go over it one more time," he said. "Remember, the bag has a red handle. The kid could have left it anywhere. But Nigel may not be in the bag any-

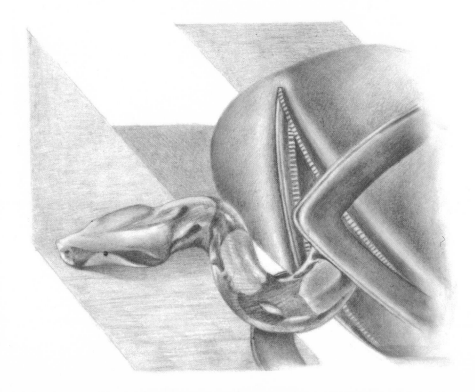

more. If he got out, there're two kinds of places he'd like: warm, dark ones, and ones that have vibrations."

"What's *vibrations*?" little Peter piped up.

"Tremors, Petey," Dorothy answered. "Like with earthquakes."

"Or like radiators," Bob explained. "When they're on."

"Shhh," hissed Martin, putting his finger to his lips. "Now, the most important thing is to find Nigel before anyone else does. We don't want a riot on our hands, and we don't want Nigel to get hurt. When snakes are out in the open, they're really vulnerable. He could get stepped—"

"What's *vulnerable*?" Petey asked.

"*Vulnerable* means easily hurt, Peter," Martin said. "Now the other thing is that we have to look for Nigel, but we can't *look* like we're looking or the librarian will start asking questions. And we know how grown-ups feel about snakes."

Everyone nodded gravely.

"I'll just tell her I'm looking for my mother," Peter said.

"Under the radiators in dark corners?" Eileen asked sarcastically.

"I think I'll say I've lost my Yankee cap," said Eli.

"Then you better take it off your head and stick it in

[38]

your pocket, dummy," said Eileen. "Unless you have two of them."

"Okay, okay," Martin whispered. "You can figure it out later. Laura and Lucy, you take the first floor. Petey, you go with Dorothy and cover the second floor. Eli and Eileen, you stay here on the third level. Bob and I'll cover the basement. That way I can keep an eye on the show and maybe get a chance to talk to Scot."

"But, Martin," said Laura. "There's just one problem. . . ."

"What's that?" Martin asked.

"What do we do if we *find* him?"

"Oh," said Martin. "Well . . ."

"It's easy," said Dorothy. "You just pick him up gently like Martin did this morning, and he'll go right around your arm. Then you put your coat over him so nobody can see."

"That's right!" Martin whispered. "Now when you hear the chimes in the clock tower, everybody back downstairs. We'll meet at the doorway to the show."

"But what if nobody finds Nigel?" Bob asked.

Martin looked at him.

"Somebody has to," he said unhappily. "Somebody just has to!"

CHAPTER

5

"Now you listen to me, Adam baby," said Max, the library custodian, to the plumber. "You get over here on the double and go to work! We've got to clean out those pipes once and for all!"

Max was using the telephone in the director's office. It was a beautiful room with a thick dark-green carpet that felt like grass under his feet, an antique cherry-wood desk, a big set of glassed-in shelves that held the library's rare-book collection, and a huge gilded mirror over the fireplace.

As he talked, Max looked at himself in the mirror.

Suddenly he realized there was something looking back at him, something that was crawling slowly and steadily along the edge of the mantelpiece—something that looked a lot like a very big snake. Max stared, his eyes popping.

"Hey, Max, you still there?" the plumber's voice came over the phone. "What'sa matter? You seen a ghost? Hey . . ."

"Yeah, yeah, I'm here," gulped Max. "But you're not gonna believe this. There's a . . . there's a . . ."

He looked back at the mirror again, but nothing was there. Max scratched his head. Then all at once he started to laugh. There in the mirror was the reflection of the telephone cord wiggling back at him! What he'd thought was a snake must have been only the twisted black cord! How could he have been so stupid?

Boy, are you an idiot, Max, he said to himself. This is a library, old buddy, not a zoo.

"Hey, Max!" the plumber was shouting. "What's going on over there? Are you all right?"

"I'm not sure," Max answered, glancing around uneasily. "You know, I think I could use a little vacation. . . ."

Suddenly there was a tremendous racket outside the office door. Someone was shrieking, and he could hear the sound of footsteps running.

[41]

"Listen, Adam baby, I gotta go. There's a big commotion outside. Somebody probably thinks he saw a snake or something."

Max hung up and hurried out. He ran smack into a girl with short black curly hair and apple-green jeans who was jumping up and down and shouting.

"But I saw it! He ran right across my atlas—right across it!"

Oh, boy, Max murmured to himself. Here we go again. Everybody's seeing snakes!

He got the excited girl to calm down and tell him exactly what had happened.

"Well," she said, a little embarrassed. "I was doing my report on Paris for school. That's for my social studies class. We're working on Europe, you know. The capital cities—"

"Right, okay," said Max. "But what happened?"

"Well, I was looking at this map of Paris in this big atlas when it just ran right across the Seine River!"

"*What* ran across the river? What do you mean 'it'?"

"The mouse! It was a spotted mouse. I'm sure of it. Brown and white. Right across the middle of Paris!"

"Oh," said Max, heaving a sigh of relief. "I thought you meant a snake. Now if it's only a mouse—"

"*Only* a mouse!" the girl cried. "In a public library? In the middle of Paris?"

"This library is not in Paris, young lady. It's in New York."

"I know it's in New York! Look, you have to catch it!"

"Right," said Max. "I'll get right on it. Let me get my broom and then you show me where you were sitting, okay?"

The girl nodded. A snake indeed! she thought to herself. How ridiculous can you get?

CHAPTER

While the twins combed the stacks on the first floor and Dorothy and Petey checked the radiators on the second floor, Eli and Eileen were crawling under tables and chairs in the reading room up on the third floor. But Martin and Bob had the most ticklish job. They were groping their way through the gloomy boiler room in the basement, examining the hissing, gurgling steam pipes and getting covered with dust and grease.

From time to time, they heard music:

[45]

I'm going to lay down
  my sword and shield
Down by the riverside
Down by the riverside . . .

The listening room was in the basement, too. A young man known as Bennie the Banjo was listening intently to a record. Bennie had a tortoiseshell comb stuck in the back of his hair. He wore a green sweatshirt with I LOVE KERMIT in black print across the front, and a pair of cowboy boots with pointed toes. The record player was in a cubby next to him, and he wore a pair of earphones.

With one hand, Bennie was taking notes in a big ringbinder notebook. With the other hand, he tapped out the beat of the music on the edge of the table.

I ain't going to study war no more
Ain't going to study war no more . . .

Bennie the Banjo loved music. Any kind of music. Folk songs, rock 'n' roll, old Broadway show tunes, dixieland, Mozart, John Cage. You name it; he'd listen to it. Bennie played the banjo in a high-school folk-rock group that gave concerts at school shows and played at private parties. He came to the library every afternoon to study different kinds of folk songs and get new material for his group.

Bennie put down his pencil, closed his eyes, and leaned back in his chair. Already he could imagine what a great arrangement his group would do with this song. He was so lost in thought that he never even noticed that his hand was tap-tap-tapping out the beat on the back of a boa constrictor. Nigel had slithered up, drawn by the vibrations coming from the record player, and settled himself comfortably on the trembling table next to it.

Tap-tap-tap-tap went Bennie the Banjo's hand. Flick-flick-flick went Nigel's tongue. He was checking his directions before moving on. He didn't like having someone use his back as a bongo drum.

Just as Nigel slipped around the edge of the table, Bennie the Banjo opened his eyes. He almost jumped out of his chair. In fact, if he hadn't been wearing earphones plugged into the record player, he'd have gone through the ceiling! Because right there, staring at him from around the corner of his notebook, was a real live boa constrictor!

"Hey, man," Bennie said out loud. "I just don't believe this. I must be going bananas! Too many late nights and too much heavy music . . ."

[47]

He leaned back in his chair again and closed his
eyes, then opened them again and looked at the table.
Nigel was gone.

"Yeah, man," said Bennie. "I think I better just finish
out this side and then go on home and take a nice long
nap. Snakes in the library—oh, brother . . ."

Bennie didn't see Martin standing in the doorway,

studying the record player. He and Bob had emerged emptyhanded from the boiler room. They'd even tried the humming Coke machine down the hall and the librarian's typewriter, although it wasn't an electric one. Nothing. But a record player should send out the right kind of vibrations for boas.

"How long are you going to use that?" Martin asked, speaking as loudly as he dared in order to be heard through the earphones. Bennie didn't answer. Martin could see it was hopeless. Judging from the pile of records next to Bennie, Martin thought he'd be there a pretty long time.

Martin decided he'd better check back periodically. He couldn't really search while Bennie the Banjo was around.

CHAPTER

7

"In there! He went in there!" the girl with the atlas shrieked, jumping up on a chair and pointing toward the wall.

"Where? Where?" shouted Max, rushing up with a broom.

"In there! In that machine right over there!"

"In the *Xerox* machine?" Max asked dumbly, his mouth open. He stared at the machine and scratched his head. The cover had been left open, and there was a stack of manuscript pages next to it. Whoever was doing the copying had obviously taken a break, but Max still couldn't figure out what a mouse would be doing in the machine. "Are you sure?"

Several readers had left their seats and come running to see what all the fuss was about. Dorothy and little Peter interrupted their search in the stacks and hurried over, too. They had a feeling Nigel might be at the center of things. Everyone gathered around the Xerox machine and began to talk excitedly.

"What's going on?" Dorothy asked a large woman in a flowered dress who was standing next to her.

"They say there's a mouse in the Xerox machine," the woman explained, laughing.

"Oh, thank goodness," Dorothy exclaimed with a sigh of relief.

"Thank goodness?" the woman echoed, staring at her.

"There he goes again!" someone shouted.

"Don't let him get away!" shouted the woman in the flowered dress, trying to hit the scurrying creature with her handbag.

With Max in front waving his broom, the crowd raced off in hot pursuit.

"Hey, Dorothy," Petey whispered, taking a sheet of paper out of the machine. "Look at this."

"Get away from the machine, Petey!" Dorothy hissed.

"We're not supposed to touch it. And we've got to keep looking for Nigel."

"But, Dorothy," Peter said. "Nigel's here! He's right here!"

"What are you talking about? Right *where*?"

"On this paper!" cried Petey, handing her the sheet.

Petey was right. For there, printed on the last piece of paper to come out of the Xerox machine, was a perfect photograph of a curled-up boa constrictor!

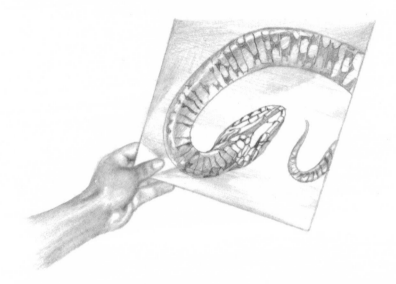

While Dorothy and little Peter gaped at the photograph, Eileen and Eli were getting discouraged up on the third floor.

"I don't know where else to look," Eileen sighed. "We've done the shelves, the tables, the chairs. We've been in the closets and behind the water fountain. We even checked in between the radiators and the walls. What are we going to do now?"

"I wonder how the others made out?" Eli said glumly, plopping into a chair. "All I got out of it was three Bazooka wrappers, two rusty jacks, and an ace of spades."

"I found a red sneaker," said Eileen, holding it up by the shoelace. "How can you lose a sneaker in a library?"

"The same way you lose a boa constrictor, I guess," said Eli.

"We've just got to think of something," Eileen sighed again, sitting down opposite Eli at the table. "We can't just give up!"

"Well, I give up," said Eli, rocking back and forth on two legs of his chair. "Martin should've bought a guinea pig. They just sit around like rocks and grunt a little and eat peanut butter sandwiches."

"Oh, c'mon, Eli," Eileen protested, exasperated. "Guinea pigs don't eat peanut—"

But Eileen never got to finish her sentence, because Eli had tried one rock too many. With a loud crash, he'd gone over backwards in his chair.

[53]

"Oh, brother!" said Eileen, jumping up. "You okay down there?"

"Yeah, I'm okay," Eli groaned from underneath the table. "But you'll never guess what's down here with me! How did we miss this, anyway?"

"Not Nigel?" Eileen whispered, glancing over her shoulder.

"Nope. Not Nigel. But you're close."

"C'mon, Eli, stop fooling around. Tell me!"

"Nigel's little nest, that's what. The big brown bag."

As Eli talked, he slowly raised his hand until it crept over the edge of the table. Eileen gasped. The hand was holding Martin's bowling bag!

"Wow!" Eileen whispered. "Hey, did you look inside?"

"Are you kidding?" said Eli, his head popping up over the rim of the table. He held out the bag to Eileen.

"I found the nest," he said. *You* find the bird."

Eileen took a deep breath, unzipped the bag all the way, and peered inside. Then she gingerly stuck her hand through the opening. After what seemed like an hour, it touched bottom.

"No Nigel," she announced, a little relieved. "Now what do we do?"

Just then the clock tower chimes began to ring.

"We go find the others, that's what we do," said Eli. "Let's pick up Dorothy and Petey on the way down. Maybe they had better luck."

Eileen and Eli walked downstairs to the second floor, where they met Dorothy and little Peter just coming out of the science fiction section.

"Hey, Eli!" Petey cried, waving a sheet of paper in the air. "Look at this!"

"*Un*-real!" said Eli. "Who took Nigel's picture?"

"The Xerox machine did," Dorothy answered matter-of-factly.

"It had vibrations, didn't it?" Peter asked, hopping up and down. "Hey, whatcha got there?"

"Martin's bowling bag," said Eileen. "Minus Nigel."

"Uh-oh," said Dorothy. "We better go find the others. Martin's going to be a nervous wreck."

The four continued down the steps to the children's level and began searching for the twins.

"There they are!" cried Petey, rushing over to Lucy and Laura. "Didja find him?"

"Shhhhhh!" Lucy hissed. "Not so loud!"

"No sign of him," said Laura, chewing on the end of her pigtail and looking worried. "We looked every-where. Even in the bathrooms. Martin isn't going to be very happy."

As the gang headed for the basement stairs, a little girl in yellow overalls jumped up and ran over to the picture-book shelf.

"Let's read this big one, Mommy!" she cried, tugging at the back of a very large book. As she pulled it off the shelf, the books next to it toppled over.

"Ooooooooh, Mommy!" the little girl squealed. "Look at the big bookworm!"

"I've told you, dear," her mother answered wearily, "there're no such things as bookworms. It's just a name for people who read lots of books. Isn't she cute?" she said to Eli. "She has such a vivid imagination! Bookworms!"

Bookworms, Eli muttered to himself as he caught up to the others at the top of the stairs. Oh, brother . . . *Oh, brother!* BOOKWORMS! Like in book-*snakes*?

"Hey, gang," he shouted, "I think we've just found Nigel!"

CHAPTER

8

The chimes had stopped ringing five minutes ago, and Martin was getting impatient. He and Bob stood next to the door, glancing nervously back and forth between the zoo show inside and the stairs opposite. They'd searched high and low all over the basement. Martin had even gone back to the listening room three times to check the record player. Bennie the Banjo had been replaced by a young man in a white toga who sat on the floor in the lotus position listening to yoga exercises. Maybe yoga just didn't have the right vibrations for Nigel, Martin said to himself.

He looked at the stairs again. Where was everyone? Maybe they'd all given up and gone home? No, he thought, real friends stuck by you when things got rough. Then he stole a glance at Scot, who raised his eyebrows in a question and motioned him to come inside.

Martin shrugged sadly and was about to go in and explain when he heard what sounded like buffalo stampeding down the stairs. He whirled around and there they were: Lucy and Laura and Eli and Eileen and Dorothy and little Petey. They all rushed up to Martin, laughing and shouting and slapping him on the back and jumping up and down.

"We got him! We got him!"

"There was this girl—"

"—and a mouse—"

"—in the Xerox machine!"

"With the bookworms, for heaven's sake!"

Martin couldn't figure out what they were talking about. He took two steps backward and let out an ear-splitting whistle. The gang fell silent immediately, and all the people in the auditorium spun around in their seats and stared. Scot almost dropped his tagoo.

"FAN-tastic!" Martin said, breaking into a broad grin. "You are all *fan*-tastic! You can tell me the whole story later, but now I gotta give Nigel to Scot. I mean, you *do* have him, don't you?"

"Where's the bag?" asked Dorothy, looking around. "Who's got the bag?"

"Lucy has it," said Laura.

"No I don't. *You* do," said Lucy.

"I do *not*!" said Laura. "Eli must have it."

"I haven't got it!" Eli protested. "Eileen was carrying it."

"I was not!" shouted Eileen. "I never had it."

"It's okay, everybody," beamed little Peter. "*I* got it! Here, Martin," he said, handing over the bowling bag. "Hey, you can have this picture of Nigel, too. I bet no-body'll b*elieve* it!"

"Thanks, Petey," said Martin, laughing. "And thank you, everyone! Now let's go in. Nigel's got a show to do!"

Late that afternoon, when Martin brought Nigel home from the library, he found his mother sitting at the kitchen table, drinking a glass of lemonade. She looked tired, and a little cross. Martin hoped she hadn't heard about the library adventure. What if she made him take Nigel back to the pet shop?

"Hi, Mom," he said, trying to smile. "What's happening?"

Martin's mother put down her glass and looked at him.

"How was the show?" she asked. "Did everything go all right?"

"Oh yeah, sure!" Martin gulped. "It was fine."

"Well, I'm glad you had a good afternoon," his mother replied, taking another sip of lemonade. "Because I haven't."

"What's wrong?" asked Martin timidly, fearing the worst.

"Wrong? Everything's wrong, that's what. I've been on the phone all day fixing things with the neighbors. You can't believe the dumb things people say. Well, I guess parents have trouble sometimes believing what their kids tell them. Bob's father threatened to call the police! Can you imagine? He thought boa constrictors were poisonous!"

Martin was amazed. Could this be his mother talking?

"And the twins' mother was practically hysterical about her girls getting squeezed to death! She was going to report Nigel as a health hazard!"

"What did you tell her?" Martin asked.

"Why," his mother replied, "I said the great thing about boas is they don't wake up the neighbors in the middle of the night and they don't turn over trash cans or dig up gardens—remember?"

Martin's face broke into a wide smile. "Yeah," he said. "Thanks, Mom."

"And they only eat about once a month. Which reminds me—just when during the month *does* Nigel eat?"

"Oh, brother!" said Martin, slumping into a chair. "I forgot to ask. But that's okay," he added, brightening. "All we have to do is offer him a mouse—or two or three. And see if he takes it! No spotted ones, though. The man in the pet store says he won't eat the spotted kind."

"Well, I guess that makes things a little simpler, doesn't it?" His mother smiled ruefully. "But just where do you plan on getting this mouse . . . or two or three?"

Martin put his elbows on the table, cupped his chin in his hands, and looked up at his mother.

"Well, I *do* have an idea. . . ."

"Yeeeess?"

"I thought maybe we could put Nigel in the basement. He'd be a whole lot better than a mousetrap."

"You mean you think he can catch his own dinner? That's not a bad idea. As a matter of fact, if we were really smart, we'd start a service. Can you see it? Boa Exterminators, Inc.!"

"I don't know about that, Mom," Martin said. He picked up the bowling bag and headed for the stairs.

"Right now I think I better put Nigel in his aquarium and let him get some sleep. He sure has had one rough day!"

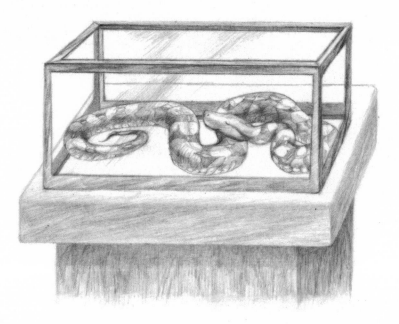